A Hare-Raising Tail

A Fletcher Mystery

A Hare-Raising Tail

by Elizabeth Levy
Illustrated by Mordicai Gerstein

Aladdin

New York London Toronto Sydney Singapore

First Aladdin edition May 2002
Text copyright © 2002 by Elizabeth Levy
Illustrations copyright © 2002 by Mordicai Gerstein

ALADDIN PAPERBACKS
An imprint of Simon & Schuster Children's Publishing Division
1230 Avenue of the Americas, New York, NY 10020

Designed by Lisa Vega
The text of this book was set in ACaslon Regular

Printed in the United States of America
10 9 8 7 6 5 4 3 2 1

The Library of Congress Catalog Card Number: 2001096536
ISBN 0-689-84626-6 (Aladdin pbk.)

Contents

One

Two

Three

Four

Five

Six

One

Love is the Biggest Mystery of All

Just because I'm a sleepy-eyed basset hound doesn't mean I don't have a very big brain. With my brain cells I can solve mysteries and tell tales that will make your hair stand on end. Speaking of a tale with a hare in it, you'll meet Aniken, the nasty rabbit in question, soon.

First let me introduce you to my three best friends—two are human. One is a flea. To some people my friendship with a flea may sound mysterious or weird. It is to me, too.

I was born a purebred basset hound. My first few weeks with Mom were warm and milky, and I was happy. My mom worried about me more than

ME AS A PUPPY

the other pups, though. I was born with a stubby tail. Basset hounds are supposed to have long, sweeping tails. Mom said that meant that I'd never make it in the dog-show world.

The day before my brothers and sisters and I were shipped to a pet store, Mom told me to be proud of my unusual markings. Maybe you didn't notice them?

All my brown spots are in the shape of the continents. Did it do me any good? At the pet store, humans picked little fluff balls when there I was with the whole map of the world on me. One by one my brothers and sisters found homes. Not me.

After a few months the pet-store owner needed room in the window for the younger pups. I got kicked out the back door. I was on the streets. I was on my own.

As the weather got colder my life became more miserable. I ate some things that embarrass even me. Then there were the fleas. I was scratching one day when I heard a voice in my ear say, "Hey, that hurts."

It was the first time I had heard a flea talk.

"Get out of my ear!" I told him.

"My name is Jasper. I'm just out of the cocoon. Give me a break."

"Why should I?"

"Look, suppose we make a deal. I'll tell all the other fleas to leave. What's one flea? You're a big dog."

I sighed. "Can you really get rid of the others?" I asked him. "All the fleas I know travel in crowds."

"I am not an ordinary flea."

"I am not an ordinary dog," I said. "And it hasn't done me much good. No human wants me."

"Well, I do," said Jasper, perched right above Italy on my ear.

"Sure, you're a flea. Fleas always want dogs."

"I could entertain you," said Jasper. "No jaguar jumps in the jungle like Jasper."

JASPER ON MY EAR JUST ABOVE ITALY

"I can see you like tongue twisters," I said.

"I like anything that twists," said Jasper. He did a triple flip from one ear to the other.

"That was quite spectacular," I had to admit.

"If I were a four-foot-tall human, I could jump over a twenty-story building. Jumping Jack Jasper at your service."

"I don't need a flea," I said. "I need a human to take care of me. I'm looking for one about eight or nine years old. They're old enough to take me for walks and feed me, and young enough to have time for snuggling. Jumping is not something I'm interested in."

"We can be a team. I'll do the jumping. You do the lying down. Did you know I can jump thirty thousand times without stopping?"

He started jumping from one side to the other. It tickled. But I have to admit, with each jump he must have said something to the other fleas, because one by one they left.

Jasper settled back down near my ear. "I told the others to find their own dog. It's you and me. What's your name?"

"I don't know yet. My mother told me I'd know the right one when a human said it. It's one of the trade-offs. We let them name us—they feed us and cuddle us for life."

Suddenly Jasper yelled, "Watch out!" but it was too late. Something large and stringy landed on us both. We were trapped.

"He looks like a stray," I heard a human voice say. My mom had warned me to never let humans think I was a stray. But what could I do? I was caught in a net and so was Jasper.

Why do people call it a shelter? It was crowded with more dogs and cats than I had ever seen in one place before. The noise, the noise, it was driving me crazy. I could barely sleep with all the yapping.

And I was worried. Humans came and went, but once again, nobody picked me. Mom warned me that if I ever found myself in a shelter I had to get out in three days—or else. She never told me what that "or else" was, but I knew it wasn't good.

My three days were almost up. "Jasper, it's time to leave me," I said. "Jump to one of those other dogs. Save yourself."

"Wait, we still have a chance," said Jasper. "Look at those two young humans who just came in. They're exactly the age you were looking for. Go up and smile at them." One of the girls was a redhead with a big smile. The dark-haired one had braces and looked more serious.

"Jill?" asked the mother. "Do you see one you like?"

"You know, Jill," said the dark-haired one. "As your best friend, I'm glad you brought me along. I know lots about picking out a good dog—think of what a great pet Bernie is."

Jill stared at her. "Gwen, Bernie's your goldfish. Goldfish aren't anything like dogs."

Gwen ignored her. "Look for one that swims in

quick circles and doesn't look bored."

"I'm not looking for a dogfish."

"I've got a list," said Gwen, taking out a piece of paper.

"1. Big bright eyes." I widened my eyes.

"2. Damp, cool nose." Jasper tried to fan my nose while I gave it a quick lick with my tongue.

"3. Lots of energy." I wiggled my whole body.

"4. Doesn't flight."

"Does she think dogs fly?" I asked Jasper. Then I realized that because Gwen wore

WIGGLING BODY   WIDE EYES

LICKING TONGUE

braces, her *F*'s come out funny. She was looking for a dog who didn't fight, not one who didn't fly.

A skinny dog pushed her way in front of me. I kept my temper and didn't growl. In fact, I lay down. My eyes started to close.

"Keep awake," shouted Jasper. "Run around a little. Remember, that's what they're looking for."

"Running around just isn't me," I said.

"You want to get out of here, don't you?" urged Jasper.

I gave it a whirl. I did a little dance. The problem was the other dogs were jumping and yelping in front of me. Who can blame them? They all wanted a home.

Gwen kept bossily pointing out the dogs that Jill should get. None of them was me. "Look how high that one jumps," she said about Brittany Spearpoint. That girl is part miniature greyhound.

"I don't want a dog thinner than I am," I heard Jill's mother say under her breath. "It would be like having a fashion model in the house."

"How about that one?" asked Gwen, about a terrier with a high-pitched yip.

Jill shook her head. Jill's mother looked relieved.

I have to admit I was really worried. I thought these girls were never going to choose me.

Then a miracle happened. "Hey," said Gwen, tapping her teeth with one hand and pointing to me with the other. "That one looks like the planet earth." She pointed to the edge of the cage, where I was lying.

CLOSE-UP OF GWEN
TAPPING HER BRACES

Jill reached her finger in and gently touched my ear. I loved the feel of her fingers. "He's got Italy on his ear, the home of pasta and pizza," said Gwen. My rear end started to twitch.

"He's a wagging globe," said Jill. "Here, little globe!"

"He's a canine geography lesson," shouted Gwen. "Mrs. Neville will love him."

My big brown eyes looked straight at Gwen and Jill. It was one of those moments. I know it sounds sappy, but I felt as if our hearts met.

Then I closed my eyes. I had been disappointed before. Other humans had looked at me and then picked someone else.

"He went back to sleep," said Gwen. "That's a bad sign. I don't think you should pick him." Then Gwen took out a sandwich. It was the first time I had ever smelled the rich, spicy, juicy smell of salami. It changed my life forever. I uncurled myself. My short stubby tail wagged back and forth to beat the band. Gwen took out a piece of salami from her sandwich and handed it to me. I swallowed it and licked her fingers. She giggled.

"I think he's the one you should get," Gwen said.

"Me too!" said Jill. "Mom, can we take him?"

"This is a very important decision," said Jill's mother. "You'll have this dog a long time—you'll probably still have him in high school."

Gwen and Jill looked at each other and then at me. "He's the one!" they repeated.

Jill's mother smiled. "Well, I like him too. I like a dog that's a little chubbier than I am."

"The moment that a human and a dog choose each other is one of the great mysteries of the universe," I said to Jasper.

"Just don't leave me behind," said Jasper. "Wherever you go, I go."

Two

The Life of a Flea Can Be Fleeting

So life began with the first humans I ever knew well. I lived at Jill's house, but Gwen came over so often that I really felt as if I belonged to the two of them. In fact, I loved them both.

I didn't feel that way about all of Jill's friends. I would soon learn that eight-year-olds travel in packs much the way dogs do.

"This is our new dog," Jill said proudly.

"What's his name?" asked Isabella.

"We don't know yet," said Jill. "I'm waiting for

the perfect name to come to me."

"He kind of looks like Garfield," suggested Chris.

"He's sure tubby enough to be Garfield," said Chris's older brother, James, which I didn't think was a terribly nice thing to say.

"If you let yourself be named after a fat cat, you'll never live it down," warned Jasper.

"What can I do? I told you. Humans have the right to name us. Still, you want a name that fits."

Gwen's and Jill's friends came up with names like Butterball, Fatso, and Tub of Lard.

"Tub of lard," whispered Jasper. "That sounds tasty."

"Not as a name," I hissed. "I do not want to have humans shouting, 'Here, Tub of Lard. . . .'"

ME, AS A TUB OF LARD

Just then Jill's mother

came outside and said, "Hi, kids, does anybody want a snack?" I'd worry about my name later. I trotted after them into the kitchen. Jill's mother started to make peanut butter sandwiches.

I patiently sat under the table waiting for something to fall my way. Someone dropped a brown blob. The taste was good, but it stuck to my mouth. I couldn't open it for a second.

I was desperately trying to clear my tongue, when I heard a boy ask "Is there any salami?" Because I was under the table, I couldn't tell which one of them said it.

"Salami and peanut butter . . . yuck!" said Jill. She is a wonderful girl, but she knows nothing about food.

I wondered which kid had asked for such a mouth-salivating treat. I was sure the peanut butter

P-NUT BUTTER+
SALAMI

would taste better with salami. Everything tasted better with salami.

All too soon the kids wanted to play outside again, even though it was cold. I was ready for a nap in the warm kitchen, but apparently I was expected to go with them. Jill put her hand on my collar. "Come on, boy," she said. "Maybe the cold air will give me an inspiration for your name."

Personally, I thought inspiration could come in a warm kitchen, but what did I know about the minds of young humans? I lay down on the front porch.

"I wish it would snow," said Chris. "If we don't get snow, how are we going to have the winter festival?"

"They're getting a snowmaking machine this year," said James.

"What's a winter festival?" asked Jasper.

"I don't know," I admitted. "If you ask me,

there's nothing very festive about winter. I hate it. Who needs snow?"

"Apparently they do."

"That dog's too lazy," said Isabella, looking at me.

"No, he's not," said Gwen. "Come on, Boy, fetch." Except, with her braces on, it came out "Fletch." She shook a stick in my face. Not a pepperoni stick, mind you—but just a stick from a tree. Here I was with a bunch of third graders who had more energy than they knew what to do with, and they wanted *me* to run after a stick. They're the ones with all the pep. I should be throwing a stick to them.

"He's not a fletcher," said Gwen. Once again *F* came out *Fl.*"

But I liked the sound of the word. It's a secret that all pets share. Most of the time we actually pick our own names. We hear a word we like, and we get humans to think *they're* giving it to us.

I jumped up and put my front paws on Jill and licked her face. She giggled. "I think he wants to be called Fletcher," Jill shouted, understanding me perfectly. And so I got my name.

"Fletcher," repeated Jasper. "Fletcher fits your face and figure and feet. Fletcher and his flea. I like it."

"You like anything that starts with the same letter. You think you can make it into a tongue twister," I said. "But you're right, 'Fletcher and his fit-as-a-fiddle, flitting flea' does have a certain ring."

A little while later the other children went home, but Gwen stayed around. Jill took me back inside.

"Mom, we named him," said Jill. "His name is Fletcher."

"Fletcher," repeated Jill's mother. "I like it. Well, Fletcher, I think it's time for a bath. I'll get the antiflea shampoo they gave us."

"ANTIFLEA!" Jasper panicked.

"Shh," I warned him. "They'll hear you."

"I'm allergic to that stuff. You've got to stop them."

There was very little I could do. Gwen and Jill got hold of my collar and dragged me into the bathroom. I couldn't think of what I could do to save Jasper. I saw a little rubber ducky sitting on the bathtub ledge.

"Flee! Jump to the duck!" I hissed to Jasper.

JASPER

RUBBER DUCK

Just then Jill's mother came in carrying a bottle. "Here it is," she said. "I know Fletcher doesn't want fleas." Oh, how I wished that humans could understand more than they did. There was no way to explain to them that this one flea was different. I looked around. I couldn't see Jasper. I couldn't feel him. I had no way of knowing whether he had escaped or not.

The life of a flea can be fleeting.

Gwen and Jill put some pink stuff on my fur. It smelled like bubble gum. I was hoping it would taste like bubble gum. No such luck.

I spit out the bubbles and twitched. Bubbles went flying everywhere. I hoped they missed Jasper.

"Hey!" shouted Jill. "He looks like a snow globe!" She laughed. It wasn't that funny.

When the soap was out of my eyes, I looked around to see if Jasper had survived the sprinkling of the flea shampoo.

"We should show him as a snow globe for the winter carnival," said Gwen. "We could make a round plastic cover for him and sprinkle soap suds down if there's no snow."

"Very cool," said Jill. "Let's take him to school

(JASPER)

for show-and-tell and tell them it's our project."

The words "show" and "tell" worried me, but not as much as I was worried about Jasper. I had no idea if he was alive or dead.

I heard a tiny sneeze, somewhere near my tail. "Jasper?" I whispered urgently.

"That was close," wheezed Jasper.

"Are you okay?" I asked.

"I'd be a dead duck without that rubber ducky," he said.

"I'm so glad you're alive!" I told him.

"Isn't it cute, the little noises Fletcher makes," Jill interrupted. "It's as if he's talking to us."

I smiled at her. Humans think the world revolves around them. They don't realize the rest of us creatures are chatting away to each other as much as they are. But it's kind of sweet that they think they're the center of the universe.

After my bath Gwen went home and Jill did some homework. Finally I had time for a nap, but for the first time in a long time, I couldn't sleep.

"Stop twitching," said Jasper. "Why are you so jumpy? You're worse than me."

"While they were giving me my bath, they talked about taking me to some kind of show," I said.

"So what? You'll do very well. You have very nice ears."

"Thank you. It's not my ears that I'm worried about. It's my tail. If they take me to do a dog show, they'll find out I'm not all that a basset hound should be."

"Your tail is cute."

"Cute doesn't cut it in the dog-show world. A basset hound is supposed to have a sweeping, comma-shaped tail. It's in the manual. It's so hunters could see us in the tall grass when we were chasing rabbits."

"Personally, I can't see you chasing a rabbit."

"It's what I was bred for."

BASSET HUNTING RABBIT IN TALL GRASS

"Oh," said Jasper.

"Oh," I said. "That's all you can say."

"Well, remember I just survived a flea bath. Let's not worry about this show stuff. For all you know, it might be months away."

Then I heard a sound that I learned to love— the refrigerator door opening. I scurried into the kitchen as fast as my short legs could carry me. I told you I could move fast when I needed to.

Three

Meet a Very Nasty Rabbit

Over the weekend Gwen and Jill made something out of strips of plastic that was shaped a little like a bell. They kept measuring me and fitting it over me.

"See," said Jill. "He looks just like a snow globe."

"Let's make a computer banner," said Gwen. "AT LAST A SNOW GLOBE THAT'S REALLY A GLOBE. The judges will love it."

"Judges," I worried to Jasper. "The judges will see my stubby tail, and I won't win any ribbons."

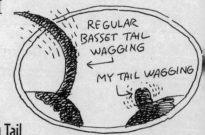

REGULAR BASSET TAIL WAGGING

MY TAIL WAGGING

The next morning Gwen came to pick up Jill for school.

"We're going to take Fletcher to show-and-tell," said Jill.

"What's the 'tell' part?" asked Jasper.

"I wish I knew," I said. "Dogs aren't allowed to tell anything at dog shows. We have to let the humans pretend they know enough to judge who's best."

I tried to hide my stubby tail under my pillow. Gwen and Jill put on my leash. There was nothing I could do.

Things only got worse the farther we walked. We ran into Chris, James, Isabella, and some more of their friends.

"Hey, why are you taking Fletcher to school?" asked Isabella.

"I'm bringing him for show-and-tell," said Jill.

"What are you going to show us—life in the fat lane?" asked Chris.

"No," said James. "She's going to show how their dog can cause an eclipse of the sun—because his gut blocks out the sun."

PLANET FLETCHER CAUSING AN ECLIPSE OF THE SUN

Jill put her hands on her hips. "My dog is not an eclipse of the sun. Fletcher is a dog with special qualities."

"Special needs, more likely," joked James. "Like you need a forklift to carry his dog food."

"We're making him into a snow globe for the winter festival," said Gwen. "We'll win hands down."

"Hey, you can't! I'm working on a snow globe," said James. "I've got an idea but I need an animal that's all white. . . . Too bad Fletcher's got those spots."

"His spots are his best feature," said Jill.

"You could use a polar bear," said Isabella.

"Right, where am I going to get a polar bear?" scoffed James. "I need something smaller than your fat dog."

"He'd never fit in a snow globe," teased Chris.

"He fits in ours," said Gwen, angrily.

I was a little hurt by all the fat jokes. Humans are very peculiar. They can be nice one on one. However, in a group, if one of them is mean, a mean germ goes around and infects everybody.

When we got to school, Jill and Gwen took me into their classroom. They put their things into their cubbyholes. I saw the teacher at the front of the room looking at me a little nervously.

"Hey, Buddy, is that a flea in your ear?" I heard

a low voice say. I knew it wasn't a human.

In the back of the room was a white rabbit in a cage. I went back to say hello.

"Hey, Dog Breath, back off," said the rabbit, twitching his ears.

"I don't appreciate being called 'Dog Breath,'" I said to the rude rabbit. I moved a little closer so that he could get a good whiff of my breath.

"That salami isn't doing any good for your breath, Sweetie."

I sniffed a little closer to the creature's cage. "Listen, Carrot Muncher, my name is Fletcher, not Dog Breath."

"Yeah, yeah, I'm sure the humans gave you that name. They call me Aniken. I'm named for a Star Wars creature. Not that anybody ever bothered to show me the movie."

"Aniken seems like a nice name for a rabbit,"

said Jasper. "It's better than Flopsy or Bugsy."

"That's just what a flea brain would say," Aniken sneered. "So what are you here for? Are you the new flavor of the day? I bet you're here for show-and-tell."

"We are. Where are the other show dogs?"

"Oh, you poor, innocent puppy," said Aniken, laughing at me and twitching his ears back and forth.

"Gwen and Jill," said a girl I hadn't met. She was standing on the far side of Aniken's cage. "I think your dog is scaring our rabbit."

"Denise, he's just making friends with Aniken," said Jill.

"As if!" sniffed Aniken, pulling himself up to his full height in his cage, his ears flopping back and forth furiously. "Rabbits and hounds cannot be friends."

"Look!" said Denise. "Aniken's shaking. I think he's scared of Fletcher. Aniken is trying to run away from that dog."

Aniken laughed. "Humans are stupid. I wouldn't be scared of a fat basset hound with a tail that looks like a bit-off hot dog."

"I don't think you're a very nice rabbit," said Jasper.

"And, personally, I'm of the opinion that the only good flea is a dead flea."

"Hey," I growled at Aniken. "That's enough. Jasper just survived a flea bath."

"That dog growled!" shrieked Denise.

"Not Fletcher!" said Gwen. "He wouldn't growl."

Aniken laughed at us.

"That is definitely one nasty rabbit," whispered Jasper. "I've got a very bad feeling about him."

Just then there was a knock at the door of the classroom. "Mrs. Neville," said James. "My teacher, Mr. Cranston, asked if he could talk to you for a moment."

"All right. Everybody, we'll have five minutes of silent reading. I'd like you all to remain quiet." She left the room, still looking at me. James glanced at the back of the room too, as if surprised to see me there, although he knew that I was coming to school. Meanwhile, I still had to worry about show-and-tell.

"Won't you tell me what this show-and-tell is about?" I pleaded with Aniken.

"Beat it," said Aniken. "There's only room for one creature in my classroom, and I'm it. I'll find some way to let those humans know that stubby-tailed basset hounds belong back in the pound."

"You wouldn't," I said.

"Oh yeah, just try me."

Mrs. Neville walked back in the room. I lifted my chin to try to make a good impression—the way that I knew show dogs were supposed to. Aniken's ears flicked back and forth, but he looked puffed up with himself, not scared.

"We brought him for show-and-tell," said Gwen and Jill.

Gwen and Jill pulled on my leash and brought me up to the front of the class.

"This is my new dog, Fletcher," said Jill. "Some of you already know him. But he is a very unusual dog."

"He scared Aniken, and he's scaring me," said Denise.

"Denise," said Gwen, sounding annoyed. "There's nothing to be scared of about Fletcher. He's the most gentle dog in the world."

I wished Gwen hadn't said that. Denise was genuinely scared, and I knew that when someone is afraid of dogs, it doesn't help to say, "Don't be afraid." Humans who are scared give off a smell that's not good. It doesn't smell like salami. It smells like something that's been lying on the ground too long.

"Mrs. Neville, we brought Fletcher in because he's a teaching tool. You told us to look for something in our everyday world that would help us learn. He's perfect."

"Yeah, he's a tool to teach you not to get fat," said Chris. A bunch of kids started laughing. Most of the time I like the sound of kids' laughter, but when it's a put-down laugh, it grates against my fur.

"He's not a fat tool," explained Jill. "Look at him."

"Gwen and Jill . . . perhaps you could get to the point of why you brought Fletcher in for show-and-tell." Mrs. Neville sounded a little impatient.

"Did you know that basset hounds are bred to hunt rabbits and other small game?" asked Denise. "I think he's disturbing Aniken." I wondered how somebody who was afraid of dogs knew so much about us.

"Look at him," said Gwen. "We didn't bring

him in to disturb Aniken. He's very special."

"Fletcher, roll into a ball," said Jill. It was a command I was very good at. I rolled into a ball. The whole class came up and looked at me.

"That looks like Florida," said Mrs. Neville, pointing to my fur. "He's got a shape that looks like Florida on his side."

"I see the Great Lakes," said Isabelle.

"I see Mexico," said Denise shyly. I rolled over so she could see more of Central and South America. Sometimes if we roll over and show our stomachs to a human who is afraid, she or he will calm down. I am very good at rolling over and showing my stomach.

"Why, he really is a teaching tool!" said Mrs. Neville. "Perhaps this afternoon, we will have our geography lesson on Fletcher."

I was the hit of show-and-tell. Who knew?

Is This the Face of a Rabbit Killer?

Later that day we had snack and recess, two of the most beautiful words in the human language. I had a great time at recess. There was a ball and a hoop on a board. The kids threw the ball up, trying to get it into the hoop. When they missed, they fetched it themselves, bumping into each other. They didn't once bother to try to get me to chase after the ball.

I took a nap. Even Jasper closed his eyes in the warm sun. Nobody paid any attention to us. I could have gone anywhere, but there was no place I wanted to go.

Then a whistle blew. Gwen and Jill came over to where I was sleeping and tugged at me. "Come on, Fletcher. We almost forgot about you."

When we went back into the classroom, there was a funny odor that hadn't been there before. Something was weird, but I wasn't sure what.

Then I heard a loud scream!

"Aniken's missing! Aniken's gone!" yelled Isabella.

"What?" demanded Mrs. Neville. She pushed her way to the back of the room.

I couldn't see. I put my front paws on a desk to try to look over the crowd.

Aniken's cage door was open. The newspapers were all messed up. There was no funny bunny.

"I bet Fletcher ate him," shrieked Denise. "You

brought a rabbit hound into the classroom. Aniken's a goner."

I widened my eyes. She couldn't believe that I would eat their rabbit. He was a nasty little hare, but I am not a killer.

Suddenly the whole atmosphere in the room changed. Everyone was looking suspiciously at me.

"Gwen and I were playing basketball, and Fletcher was sleeping during recess," stammered Jill.

"I bet he snuck back in, took Aniken, and buried him somewhere," said Chris.

They were all looking at me as if I were guilty.

Mrs. Neville sighed. "Let's not jump to any conclusions," she said. "Everybody look for Aniken. Gwen and Jill, please keep that dog on a tight leash."

Suddenly I was "that dog," a dog that needed to be kept on a tight leash.

"You know what happens to dogs that are suspected of killing other pets, don't you?" Jasper said, hysterically. "They're sent back to the dog pound. And this time, you may not be given a second chance."

"You know I didn't eat that rabbit," I said. "I'm innocent."

"Sure you're innocent," said Jasper. "But how are you going to prove it? I bet that rabbit ran away himself—just so you'd be blamed."

I wasn't sure. Rabbits have clumsy feet. Their paws are good for thumping, but if Aniken got out, he had to have had outside help. Who could have taken him?

At the end of the day, Aniken still hadn't showed up. I was worried.

"They all think it was me," I said to Jasper. "Who would want to frame me?"

"Aniken!" said Jasper.

"I told you, I don't think that rabbit busted out of here himself. Who didn't like me from the beginning? Denise. Sure, she looks like a tiny, sweet human, but she hates dogs. She could have taken Aniken, hoping that I'd be blamed."

Gwen and Jill were standing by the empty rabbit cage. Jill looked morose. Gwen was tapping her teeth nervously.

I nudged Jill on her leg. She patted me absentmindedly. I didn't need her to be absentminded. I needed her full attention.

I nudged her toward Denise.

"Keep your killer dog away from me," warned Denise. She was clutching a very lumpy backpack.

"Fletcher's not a killer," said Gwen, finally stopping tapping her braces. I lifted my paw and held my nose in the air, pointing at the backpack.

Believe me, short of making a sign that said JILL AND GWEN! LOOK IN THE BACKPACK! I couldn't do more.

Denise stuck her lower lip out. "Why is your dog doing that funny thing with his paw?"

DENISE'S LUMPY BACK PACK

"He's pointing!" said Jill.

"He's pointing towards your backpack!" exclaimed Gwen.

Denise clutched her backpack tighter.

"What do you have in there?" Jill asked.

"Nothing," said Denise. "It's nothing."

"I don't believe you," said Gwen. "I think you have a certain bunny rabbit in there."

Denise lowered her eyes. She looked guilty.

"Let's go in the closet," she said.

Gwen and Jill looked at each other. Then we all

went into the closet. Denise tried to hide behind the coats.

"There *is* a bunny in my backpack," she admitted.

I breathed a sigh of relief. A confession. The mystery was solved. Finally the rabbit would be out of the bag . . . and everyone would realize that I was innocent.

Five

Banned For Life

Well, Denise pulled a rabbit out of the bag, all right. But it was a stuffed rabbit, very well used. Its plush fur was matted. It wasn't even white. It was a dirty gray.

"Don't tell anybody that I bring Flopsy to school, will you?" she pleaded. "I've had him since I was a baby."

Jill's shoulders slumped. "We were sure you took Aniken and blamed Fletcher because you were so afraid of him."

I lowered my head. I had been sure too, but one

look at Denise's face, and I knew that she wasn't the culprit. I wished I could help her be less afraid of dogs, but I had work to do.

I knew I didn't have much time. I had to discover who had taken Aniken, and I just hoped that I'd find him alive.

Before I even had time to plot out my next move, Jill's mother was at the door. Jill whispered something to her. "Mrs. Neville?" she asked. "Is there a problem?"

"Well, I'm not sure," said Mrs. Neville. "Aniken, our rabbit, is missing."

"Mom," said Jill. "Some kids think Fletcher did it."

"Fletcher?" said Jill's mother. "That doesn't sound like him."

"Have you had him very long?" Mrs. Neville asked.

"Well, actually only about a week," said Jill's

mother. "But he's been so sweet, and he hardly moves. I can't imagine him chasing a rabbit."

Mrs. Neville sighed. "Well, maybe to be on the safe side, Jill had better keep Fletcher at home from now on. And maybe you'd better keep your eye on him. Once he's hunted small game, he might go after kittens or gerbils."

"Mom, Fletcher wouldn't do that," gasped Jill.

"I'm so sorry this happened," said Jill's mother. "I never dreamt that when Gwen and Jill said they wanted to bring Fletcher into school and talked about making him into a snow globe that it would cause this much trouble."

"A snow globe for the winter festival?" asked Mrs. Neville.

"We never got to tell you that part," said Gwen.

Gwen and Jill looked so sad as we filed out of the classroom. As we passed the empty rabbit cage

I took a sniff. With all the fuss during the day, I hadn't been able to get really near it. It wasn't a rabbitty smell. It smelled a little nutty, with just a hint of something else. Something familiar.

Jill was pulling on my leash; I took a deep whiff. I tried to keep my brain cells focused, but it was hard when I was in danger of losing the only home I had ever known.

On the drive home Jill's mother put me way in the back. Nobody talked very much. Jill's mother tried to sound cheerful.

"Let's take the weekend to think over what we should do," she said. "I'm just not sure we should keep a dog if he goes after small animals. Let's take the weekend to decide."

"Can we still take Fletcher as a snow globe to the winter festival?" asked Jill. "It's in the town park, not on school grounds. And he'll either be on his leash or in the snow globe."

"Are you sure you want to?" asked Jill's mother.

"If this is going to be our last weekend with Fletcher, I want to spend as much time with him as I can," said Jill. She sounded close to tears. So was I.

"Me too," said Gwen.

Jill's mother sighed. "All right. Gwen, when we get home, I'll check and see if it's okay for you to spend the night, and then tomorrow we'll go to the festival."

"Well at least that's a reprieve," said Jasper.

"Not much of one," I sighed. "I'm forbidden to even enter the school grounds. Wherever Aniken is, I probably have no chance of finding him."

"Don't worry. We'll work it out," chirped Jasper.

Sometimes having a buddy who's always an optimist can be very annoying.

Six

The Twitching Clue

I couldn't imagine any group less festive than ours as we tracked through the light dusting of snow to the town park. Gwen and Jill told me to lie down under their plastic top. They positioned me just under one of the snowblowers so that it looked as if I were a snow globe. Then they put out their computer sign that they had laminated.

Denise and Isabella came by. "Gosh, another snow globe," said Isabella. "James made a snow globe too."

Denise kept her distance from me. "Are you keeping that dog?" she asked. "I heard a rumor that Mrs. Neville told you to get rid of him."

"He's not allowed back at school," said Jill. "But we haven't decided what to do yet." I shivered. Something in her voice made me feel there really wasn't too much hope.

"He looks cold," said Denise. I nodded at her. For a moment, I felt she understood a little of what I was going through.

"James's globe can't be as good as ours," said Gwen. "We've got a real globe in our snow globe."

"They were just setting it up when I went by," said Denise, taking a step back from me. "I couldn't really see it, but James said it had a real surprise in it."

"Maybe I should go look," Gwen said to Jill. "You stay here with Fletcher."

Jasper's teeth were chattering. "How long does this winter festival go on?" he complained.

"Enjoy it," I said. "This may be our last day of freedom."

"My antennas are so cold, I can't feel anything," Jasper complained.

"Well, find some of my loose fur and wrap yourself in it," I suggested.

JASPER IN LEG & EAR WARMERS

"Great idea," said Jasper. He quickly knitted himself little antenna muffs and six tiny leg warmers.

Gwen wasn't gone very long.

When she came back, she was chewing something. I can hear the sound of chewing from a long way away.

I twitched my nose. The smell was familiar. Nutty, yet spicy.

"What are you eating?" Jill asked.

"Peanut butter and salami!" said Gwen. "Isabella

gave me a bite of a sandwich 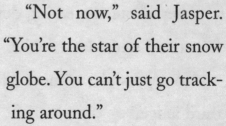 A PIECE OF SALAMI PEANUT BUTTER SANDWICH

someone gave her. Anyhow, James's snow globe isn't as good as ours. It's all white. I couldn't really see it, though, because the judges were already looking at it."

"Peanut butter and salami!" I yelped.

"Quiet, Fletcher," said Jill.

"That was the smell in Aniken's cage," I whispered to Jasper. "Somehow Aniken's disappearance is connected with whoever gave Gwen that peanut butter and salami sandwich. I've got to track them down. Basset hounds are very good trackers. We're related to bloodhounds."

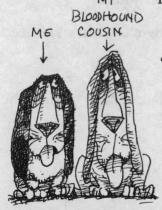
ME ↓
MY BLOODHOUND COUSIN ↓

"Not now," said Jasper. "You're the star of their snow globe. You can't just go tracking around."

"Here come the judges!" shouted Jill. "Oh, no, Mrs. Neville is one of the judges."

The judges came over to our site. "You're our last entry," said Mrs. Neville. "Don't worry, Gwen and Jill," she whispered. "I'll be fair. I know this isn't school grounds, and you worked hard on this."

The judges walked around me slowly, looking at the way I was lying under the plastic, and the way the snowflakes were falling gently on me. "Why, this is very interesting," said one. "It must be the year of the snow globe."

"He's a real globe," said Jill. "See our sign."

"Very original," said another judge.

They wrote something down. "I think we need to confer," said Mrs. Neville.

"Is it possible to move your entry?" asked the third judge.

"Oh, yes," said Gwen. "Fletcher can move when he has to."

The judges formed a little circle and whispered. I flicked my ears to try to hear, but I couldn't make out their words. It was also hard to hear because Jasper was so nervous, he was like a jumping jack.

Finally the judges split apart. "We'd like you to bring your entry up to the platform," said Mrs. Neville.

Gwen and Jill dismantled the plastic bubble. I was anxious to see what the other snow globe was. It was under the same kind of plastic cover, but it was all white. But my nose twitched. I smelled peanut butter and salami and something else.

Then I saw James. His was the other entry. I sniffed deeply. I detected a weird aroma—a mix of salami and peanut butter, with just a whiff of rabbit.

The judges went to the microphone. "Ladies and gentlemen, girls and boys. For the first time at the winter festival, we have a tie for the winning entry. They are both snow globes, and we thought we'd leave it up to the audience's applause. Our first entry is AT LAST A SNOW GLOBE THAT'S REALLY A GLOBE. You have to look closely at the dog's spots. But it is a globe within a globe!"

The audience burst into applause for me. I wagged my stubby tail. My mother would have been proud. I was at a show and I was getting applause.

"Our second entry," said the judge, "is also original. It's an all-white number."

James came onstage, carrying his snow globe. I smelled his breath. Peanut butter and salami. The smell that had been on Aniken's cage. James had been at the table the first time I had ever heard anyone ask for peanut butter and salami.

There was just a smattering of applause. "What's so original about snow in a snow globe?" shouted one of the audience members.

"I can pull a rabbit out of my globe," said James. "It's a magic globe." He reached in and pulled a rabbit out by its ears.

The audience applauded.

"Aniken!" I shrieked over the applause. "You're alive."

"Oh, my goodness," said Jasper, doing a triple flip. "We're saved."

"Hey!" shouted Gwen, tapping her braces. "That's our classroom rabbit. James took it from our classroom, and poor Fletcher got blamed."

"This isn't your rabbit," said James, putting the rabbit back into the globe. "I got him from a pet store. They had lots of white rabbits."

"Where's your receipt?" demanded Jill.

"I paid cash," James said smugly. "Who brings a receipt for a rabbit to a winter festival?"

Mrs. Neville looked closer. "I don't know," she said. "He looks a little like Aniken . . . but the truth is, rabbits *do* look alike."

"Aniken," I begged. "They're sending me back to the pound because they think I took you. I know it was James. Help me."

"Hey," said Aniken, hopping into my snow globe and giving me a dirty look. "The kid feeds me peanut butter and salami. He changes my cage. It's not a bad exchange."

"But . . . but . . ." I sputtered. I couldn't believe how unfair it was. I had the culprit, but he was going to get away with it.

Then I had an idea. "Jasper, jump!" I said.

"No, I told you before. Where you go, I go. If you go back to the pound, I'm going with you."

I whispered that if he did exactly what I told him to do, we'd be safe. It required a leap of faith. A big leap.

"Okay!" said Jasper, taking the assignment. "That jackrabbit jerk will be jiggling Jell-O."

"Enough with the tongue twisters, just jump!" I urged him.

A JELL-O JACK RABBIT JIGGLING

He did a magnificent flying flip and landed on Aniken's ear. Then he went to work, burrowing into one ear and then jumping quickly over to the other.

JASPER

Aniken's ear twitched back and forth like a metronome at a rock concert.

"It *is* Aniken,"

said Denise. "Look at his ears. That's exactly what he did when he saw Fletcher before. He's scared of Fletcher."

"That's right," said Isabella.

"The jig is up," said Gwen, tapping her braces. "James's rabbit has to be Aniken. His twitching ears prove it. James took Aniken."

Mrs. Neville looked at James. "I do remember Aniken's ears twitching when he first saw Fletcher. I believe it is Aniken. James, I think it's time for you to tell the truth."

James wouldn't look her in the eye. "All right . . .," he said. "I heard Gwen and Jill talking about a snow globe. I had already come up with the idea of an all-white snow globe. I couldn't believe my little brother's friends could come up with an even better idea. Then when I saw their classroom rabbit, I knew he'd be perfect. I didn't know the dog would

be blamed. I was going to return the rabbit to the classroom on Monday."

"Monday would have been too late," yelled Jill. "We might have taken Fletcher back to the dog pound."

"Even I wouldn't want that," said Denise. "You know what? The more I see him, the more I think Fletcher's the only dog I'm not afraid of."

I wagged my little tail and gave her a big smile. Very shyly she touched me on the ear. "Hey," giggled Jasper. "That tickles." But, of course, Denise couldn't hear him. No humans can hear a flea. They barely listen to me, and we dogs are closer to humans than any other animal.

"Gwen and Jill," said Mrs. Neville. "I owe you an apology. Maybe one day next week, you can bring Fletcher in for another geography lesson. As for you, James, you are disqualified. And I will speak to your teacher and see you and your parents in school on Monday."

"Fletcher, you're saved," said Jill, putting her arms around me. "Thanks to Gwen's and my good detective work."

Well, the truth was that I had done the detecting, and Jasper had done the work. Still, let Gwen and Jill take the credit.

How do I love Jill and her best friend, Gwen? Let me count the ways. Jill had given me a home. Gwen had given me my name. Could any dog ask for anything more? Well, yes, a little salami. And a loyal flea who loves tongue twisters. It's a good life.